Jolly Roger and the Clever Green Parrot

Story by Debbie Croft

Illustrations by Chantal Stewart

All the pirates on Jolly Roger's ship were very hungry.

They didn't have any coconuts left to eat.

"What will we do?" said Jolly Roger.

3

"If you don't feed us, Jolly Roger,
we will not work for you!"
said Little Pirate.

"**You** will have to catch some fish!"
said Big Pirate.

Jolly Roger went to get his fishing line.

Jolly Roger saw a big worm
under some seaweed on the deck.

"This worm will be good bait,"
he said, putting it
on his line.

The fish swam
right past the bait.

"We are **very** hungry now,"
said Little Pirate.

"I will try to catch some fish in this little net," said Jolly Roger.

The fish swam right under it.

Big Pirate and Little Pirate laughed and laughed.

9

"Maybe if I make a bigger net,
the fish will not swim away,"
Jolly Roger said to himself.

He tried to make a net
with some rope.

"This is no good," he said.

"I can't do it by myself."

A green parrot flew down
from the mast.

It took the rope in its beak.

It made the rope go across and back and over and under.

"That was very clever," said Jolly Roger as he helped the parrot tie a knot. "**Now** I will catch some fish!"

Jolly Roger put the big net into the water.

In no time at all, there were four big fish in it!

"Fish for lunch!" cheered the pirates.

"Now **you** can get back
to your work," said Jolly Roger.